D0389411

SCIENCE FAIR SABOTAGE

STONE ARCH BOOKS
a capstone imprint

SNOOPS, INC. IS PUBLISHED BY
STONE ARCH BOOKS, A CAPSTONE IMPRINT
1710 ROE CREST DRIVE
NORTH MANKATO, MINNESOTA 56003
WWW.MYCAPSTONE.COM

Library of Congress Cataloging-in-Publication Data
Names: Terrell, Brandon, 1978– author. | Epelbaum, Mariano, 1975– illustrator.
Title: Science Fair Sabotage / by Brandon Terrell ; illustrated by Mariano Epelbaum.
Description: North Mankato, Minnesota : Stone Arch Books, a Capstone imprint,
[2017] | Series: Snoops, Inc.
Identifiers: LCCN 2016033023 (print) | LCCN 2016035072 (ebook) |
ISBN 9781496543479 (library binding) | ISBN 9781496543516 (paperback) |
ISBN 9781496543639 (eBook PDF)
Subjects: LCSH: Science projects—Juvenile fiction. | Contests—Juvenile fiction. |
Twins—Juvenile fiction. | Brothers and sisters—Juvenile fiction. |
African American girls—Juvenile fiction. | Hispanic American boys—Juvenile fiction. |
Friendship—Juvenile fiction. | Detective and mystery stories. |
CYAC: Mystery and detective stories. | Science projects—Fiction. | Contests—Fiction. |
Twins—Fiction. | Brothers and sisters—Fiction. | African Americans—Fiction. |
Hispanic Americans—Fiction. | Friendship—Fiction. | GSAFD: Mystery fiction. |
LCGFT: Detective and mystery fiction.
Classification: LCC PZ7.T273 Sc 2017 (print) | LCC PZ7.T273 (ebook) |
DDC 813.6 [Fic]—dc23
LC record available at https://lccn.loc.gov/2016033023

BY BRANDON TERRELL

**ILLUSTRATED BY
MARIANO EPELBAUM**

EDITED BY: AARON SAUTTER
BOOK DESIGN BY: TED WILLIAMS
PRODUCTION BY: STEVE WALKER

SNOOPS INC.

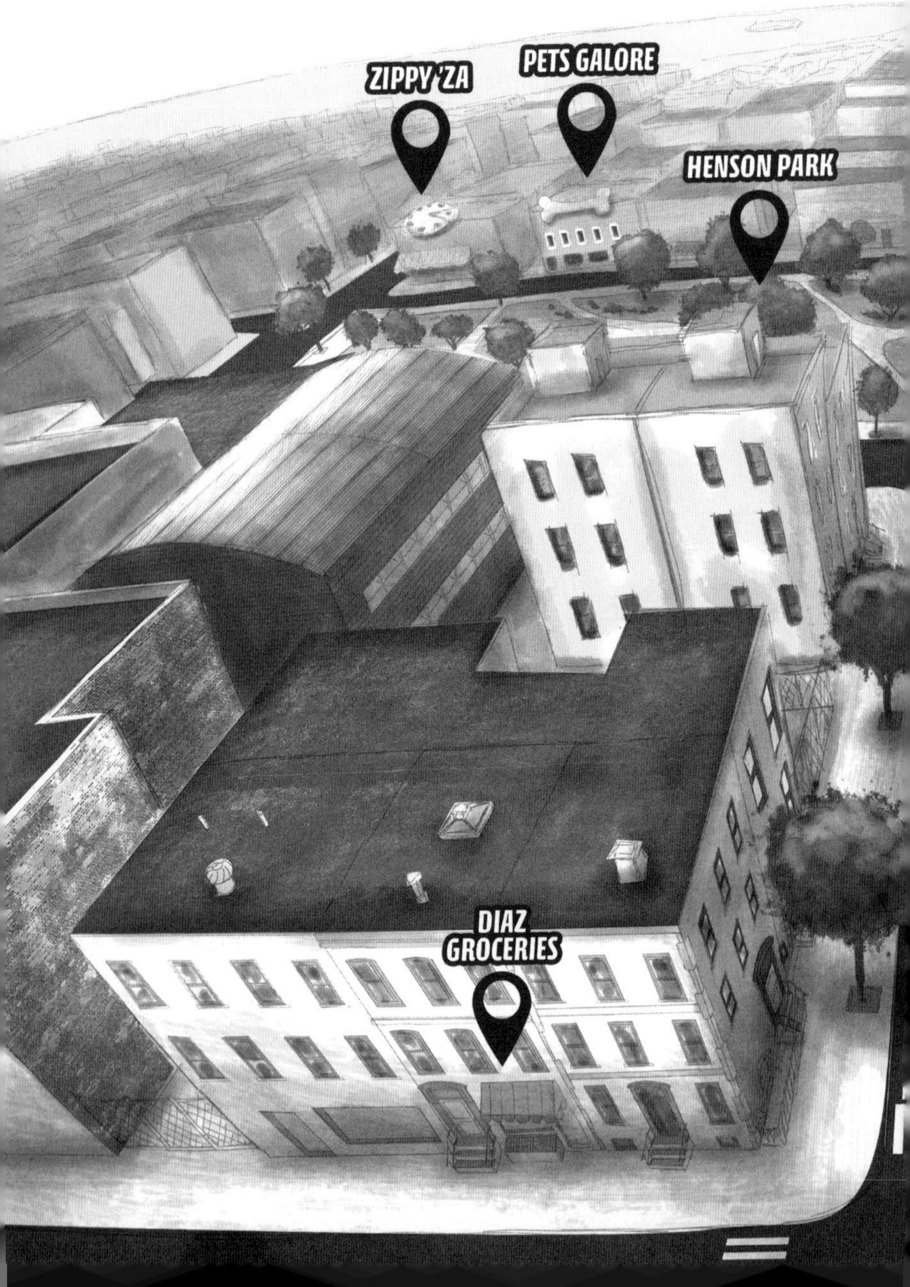

CHAPTER 1

LIFTING AND FALLING

The teenager with the baggy cargo shorts and oversized coat strolled into the grocery store with a bounce in his step. The owner of the store, a middle-aged man with short salt-and-pepper hair, gave him a smile. "Welcome to Diaz Groceries," the man said as he continued to stack bright red apples in the produce section of the store.

The teenager, wearing his earbuds, either didn't hear the man, or pretended not to. He walked with a purpose, like he knew exactly where he was going, and what he wanted. That's because he did. He always did.

The place wasn't packed, and that was perfect for his plan. There was less chance of anyone seeing him.

At the far side of the store, past the chips and crackers and juice boxes, was an aisle filled with electronics. Diaz Groceries had security cameras up front by the door. But there were none in the tucked-away back corner of the cramped store. The electronic equipment was prime for the taking.

The teen passed by a stack of tomato soup cans being built by an African-American girl with her dark hair pulled up in a ponytail. She knelt in front of the display, tagging and stacking the cans. She looked a little young to be working at the store, but the teen paid her no mind.

He cut down the bread and cereal aisle. At the far end were a brother and sister — twins, apparently, considering their matching blonde hair and scowls. They were arguing as each waved a box of cereal in front of the other.

"Choco Squares," the girl said.

"No," the boy countered. "Fruity-Wows."

"Choco Squares!"

"Fruity-Wows!"

The teen ignored them and moved on.

One row past the squabbling siblings was the electronics aisle. It held just small things, nothing major. Stuff the pawn shop over on 47th Street would pay decent money for, like battery chargers and portable hard drives. The plastic packages were barely protected . . . again. It was like the lame store owner never learned from his mistakes. The teen glanced down the aisle one way, then the other. A young man in a ball cap and a janitor uniform whistled as he pushed a bucket on wheels past the aisle.

When the coast was clear, the teen began to snitch the goods.

He stuffed his large cargo shorts and coat pockets with gear, then quickly turned to leave. He moved at the same casual pace to avoid alerting Mr. Diaz up front. As he walked to the end of the aisle, the siblings from the cereal section wheeled their metal shopping cart in front of him, blocking his path.

"Excuse me," he said.

When he looked up at the twins, he noticed the sister glance at him. She looked as if she recognized him. Like she knew what he was up to. He was just being paranoid, he had to be. Still, it wasn't worth taking a chance.

The teen turned on a heel and began to walk back the way he came.

"He's made us," twelve-year old Hayden Williams whispered.

"Way to blow our cover," her brother Jaden said.

There had to have been at least five hundred dollars worth of electronics in the teen's pockets. He was sweating. He had to get out of the store, and do it fast.

He hurried along the back of the store, hoping to reach the far end and hang a right at the wall of refrigerated coolers. By the time he was halfway past the condiments, he'd given up on playing calm. He hurried along with long strides. His stolen gear rustled and clinked in his pockets.

He didn't see the patch of wet tile floor until it was too late.

"Whoa!"

The shoplifting teen flailed his arms as he slipped along the floor. He knocked over a display of potato chip boxes and bags, and they scattered across the floor. The thief couldn't keep his balance, though. Unable to stop, he careened forward.

The girl who'd been making the tomato soup display — thirteen-year-old Keisha Turner —

stepped out from behind the last aisle. She calmly swung open one of the glass freezer doors. Billows of cold air plumed from the door as it yawned wide.

The thief couldn't stop himself. He fell, slid, and crashed right into the open refrigerator filled with TV dinners and frozen burritos. Keisha smiled. "Ouch," she said. "That's gotta hurt."

She swung the freezer door closed with glee.

Jaden and Hayden joined her. Jaden had cracked open a box of Fruity-Wow's and was munching down a handful. "Clean up in aisle six!" Jaden shouted.

"Oh, man," the janitor said as he approached. The freezer door had begun to fog up. He wiped it clear with one forearm. "Guess I forgot to put down one of those Wet Floor signs." Fourteen-year-old Carlos Diaz lifted his ball cap to reveal close-cropped curly black hair, alert eyes, and a smile as wide as his face. "What can I say? It's my first day on the job."

From inside the freezer, the shoplifter groaned. His teeth began to chatter.

The store's owner, Mr. Diaz, walked over from the produce section.

"Hey, Dad! I told you we'd snag the shoplifter who's been targeting your store. The cops are on their way," Carlos said.

Mr. Diaz slipped an arm around Carlos' shoulder and flashed a grin that matched his son's. "I had no doubt." To the shoplifter, he added, "Young man, it looks like you've been stopped cold by Snoops, Incorporated."

CHAPTER 2

SCIENCE... FAIR?

"Okay," Jaden whispered to himself, "whatever you do, don't drop the volcano."

The sixth-grader walked carefully into the gymnasium at Fleischman Middle School hefting a cumbersome, craggy model volcano in both hands. Bits of red lava were painted on the side of the stone. They dripped dramatically from the volcano's crater. At the base of the rock was a small village. Tiny villagers fled in fear of the impending eruption.

Jaden wobbled a bit as students and parents breezed past him. "Hey, watch where you're walking!" he shouted. "Mount Vesuvius coming through!"

"Relax," Hayden said from behind her brother. "You sound like someone's trying to ruin your science fair project."

The two siblings made their way through the cluttered gymnasium. Jaden held his breath as he wove toward his assigned table. He only let it out after sliding his model volcano safely onto the tabletop. "There we go," he said. He checked the small timer on the back of the volcano. It controlled when the volcano would erupt, and the amount of lava exploding out of it. Then he leaned down to adjust a bit of papier-mâché volcanic rock and two of the tiny plastic figures running in terror. "Pompeii is safe and sound. Well, for the time being. Bwa-ha-ha-ha!"

Jaden glanced up and saw the girl at the next table, Mercy Gold, giving him a funny look.

"Sorry," he said. "I'll dial back the diabolical laughing."

Rows of tables identical to Jaden's had been set up around the gym. Each had a tablecloth draped down to the floor. A large banner hung over the gym's doorway. In bold letters, the sign read: SIXTH-GRADE SCIENCE FAIR.

Jaden watched as the rest of the sixth-graders from Fleischman set up their own projects. It was the evening before the competition, but already, the tension in the air was thick. Tiny electrical gizmos whizzed on several tables. One table held a big fish tank filled with Jell-O. And poster boards with bubbly lettering sat next to many students' projects.

Hayden stopped at the table just across the row from her brother. "All right," she said. "Time to set up my project. That blue ribbon is gonna be all mine tomorrow." She placed a small device on the table, along with a cardboard tube container that held her project's blueprints in it. She'd been working on her device for weeks. As much as Jaden hated to admit it, her project put his silly volcano to shame.

Of course, Hayden had been doing that their entire lives. As siblings, the two couldn't help but be competitive. As twins, that competitiveness was dialed up even more. And it always seemed like Hayden had the edge.

"Oh, wow," Jaden heard Mercy say. "Sanjay's robot looks amazing."

A small crowd had gathered at the nearby table of Sanjay Hurkadli. Jaden stepped over to join them. Sanjay wore a crisp pink polo shirt and khakis. Placed delicately atop his head of dark, swooping hair was a funny-looking headset with a microphone snaking down to his mouth. A sleek metal robot with long, wiry arms and wide treads for feet whizzed around the table.

"Wave, Chip," Sanjay said. The robot stopped moving. One arm lifted, and fingers made of bolts, rubber bands, and wires waggled.

"Hello," the robot said, its voice a combination of electronic clicks and whirs.

The group at the table laughed. Some broke into applause.

Sanjay removed the headset and placed it on the table next to Chip. "And that's just one of the commands Chip can do," he said smugly.

While Jaden had been crafting his tiny Pompeii and its doomed citizens, his confidence had been high. Now, with each science fair project he saw, his hopes of winning sank bit by bit.

"Excuse me," a girl's voice said from behind him. "This is my table."

"Oh, sorry," Jaden said. He turned to see Britt McDaniel, a pretty girl with a smattering of freckles across her nose and cheeks. Britt had a pink backpack slung over her shoulder. A curled-up roll of blueprints stuck out of it.

Jaden moved to allow Britt access to the table beside Sanjay's.

An older boy with short brown hair, the same dash of freckles as Britt, and braces on his teeth walked alongside her. Luke McDaniel was a high school sophomore. He was one of the popular kids. Jaden had heard that last year, the yearbook committee had voted him Most Popular. Or maybe it was Best Smile . . . or Most Likely to Save Puppies From a Burning Building . . . or something like that.

Britt placed a rectangular clock on the table. "What's that?" Jaden asked.

"It's an olfactory alarm," Britt replied. "Instead of harsh beeping, it emits a pleasant smell. So you wake up happy instead of annoyed."

"You mean I could wake up to the smell of bacon cheeseburgers every day?" Jaden marveled.

Britt giggled. "Yeah, I guess."

"Cooooool!"

"Psst! Jaden!" Hayden waved him over. "Come test this out."

He walked back to his sister's table. Her device sat on the table, cobbled together from an old black computer tablet she'd found at a pawn shop. A sign written in colorful marker called it the PrintFinder Xtreme.

"Press your finger on the screen when it says to," Hayden requested as she fired up the tablet. Green lights blinked, and a small rectangle appeared in the middle of the screen. The words *Press Now* glowed above it.

Jaden pushed one finger down on the tablet.

The tablet scanned Jaden's finger. His fingerprint appeared beside the rectangle.

"Whoa," Luke McDaniel said over Jaden's shoulder. "What's that?"

Hayden blushed. "I created a fingerprinting app," she explained. "I like . . . um, detective stuff." She was flustered around the handsome tenth-grader.

Jaden rolled his eyes. *Like detective stuff?* That was putting it mildly. Hayden was Snoops, Incorporated's tech-wizard. She was even part of an online group called the Young Forensics Club. She chatted almost daily with others about various methods that detectives and police officers use to solve crimes.

"Can I try?" Luke asked.

Hayden, surprised, blurted out, "Sure!"

Jaden lifted his finger off the tablet screen, and Luke immediately pressed his down. As he did, the group that had surrounded Sanjay's table before was now crowding around Hayden. Her fingerprinting app had become the new, intriguing project to marvel at. Jaden glanced back at his own lonely-looking volcano.

A moment later, the app chirped, and Luke's fingerprint appeared on-screen. "Cool," he said.

Britt tried the app next, followed by several other science fair participants, including Mercy Gold and, shockingly, Sanjay Hurkadli. "I'm impressed, Williams," Sanjay said. The way he spoke, Jaden could tell he wasn't used to dishing out compliments.

"Thanks," Hayden said.

"I gotta jet," Jaden heard Luke say to his sister. "I'm gonna be late for work." He pointed to the Burger BOOM! logo on his shirt. The diner was just a few blocks from school. "You'll do great tomorrow," Luke told his sister. "I just know it."

"Thanks," Britt said, shyly tucking a bit of hair behind one ear.

Luke walked away, pausing at Jaden's table. "Cool volcano," he said, which gave Jaden a brief moment of pride.

The kids around Hayden's table dispersed. They returned to their own projects, preparing them for the following day's event. Jaden even saw Principal Snider, Fleischman's barrel-chested, bald principal, wandering the rows, observing students and their projects.

"Watch it. Coming through." A boy elbowed his way past Mercy and her friend as they stood chatting together. He was scowling, his brow furrowed.

"Yo, Tariq," Jaden said. "Everything okay?"

Tariq Washington didn't even stop to acknowledge Jaden. He just said, "Fine, dude. Just late. And I hate being late." As he passed by Sanjay's table, Tariq snorted rudely and added, "How's that lame bot of yours, Hurkadli?"

Sanjay puffed out his chest. "Chip is ready to take on . . . whatever you've got up your sleeve."

"Doubt it," Tariq said, claiming the only empty table left and beginning to set up.

The science fair was far more cutthroat than Jaden imagined it would be when he signed up. He thought it was going to be fun — just a silly way to make a silly volcano spray silly fake lava all over.

However, all of the other students there were acting anything but silly.

"Tomorrow's competition is gonna be brutal," Jaden muttered to himself.

CHAPTER 3
ON THE FRITZ

"Now this is what I'm talkin' about," Carlos said as he took a huge bite of his double bacon cheeseburger. Cheese oozed out and dripped onto his basket of french fries. One slice of bacon tried to escape, but the eighth-grader chomped it down.

Normally, a sight like that would have had Jaden's stomach rolling in envy. And in fact, he had the same exact Burger BOOM! classic in front of him. But for reasons that Jaden couldn't understand, he was somehow not hungry.

The quartet of Snoops, Inc. members sat in their favorite red plastic booth. Hayden had sent Carlos and Keisha a text from the school gym, and they'd met at the diner shortly after. It wasn't quite dark yet, but the sun had dipped behind some taller buildings a couple of blocks away. The light filtering in through the diner's front window was faded and gray. The neon sign in the window — OPEN 'til 10 P.M.! — glowed bright red.

"Well, I can see why you wanted to come here, Hayden," Keisha said, taking a huge sip of her milkshake. The seventh-grader was staring at the diner's counter, where Luke McDaniel was serving several customers their food.

"I know, right?" Hayden whispered, as she too gazed at Luke.

"For real?" Carlos asked through a mouthful of food. "Can you believe them, Jaden?"

Jaden was too bummed to respond. He shrugged his shoulders, plucked a french fry from his basket, and quietly chewed on it.

While the girls were distracted by Luke and his devilish good looks, Carlos leaned across the booth to Jaden. "Dude," he said. "You okay?"

"Yeah," Jaden lied. "Totally."

But he totally wasn't okay. He was still hung up on the cool projects he'd seen. Even with the timer he'd made for his volcano, his project was nothing compared to robots, fingerprint applications, and delicious-smelling alarm clocks.

In fact, the more Jaden thought about it, the more it bugged him. And it wasn't just the science fair. Looking at his friends sitting together at the booth, Jaden wasn't sure what he added to Snoops, Inc. as a detective team. Carlos was the face of the team. Keisha was the muscle. And Hayden was the brains.

But what was *he*?

The bell on Burger BOOM!'s door jingled as it swung open and a gaggle of girls waltzed in. Jaden saw Frankie Dixon with them. He'd had a crush on Frankie for as long as he could remember. He even liked her back when she and Keisha were inseparable friends. They used to hang out together in the apartment building or at Snoops HQ and whisper to each other. Now, the two barely talked to each other, thanks to an incident Keisha only called The Fallout.

Jaden slid out of the booth. "Later, guys," he said.

"Where ya goin'?" Carlos asked.

"Home. I'm tired. Big day tomorrow."

As Jaden began to walk toward the door, he heard Frankie gasp and say, "There he is!" Her friends, all members of the school's spirit squad, were decked out in Fleischman Bulldogs shirts and shorts.

Jaden stopped. Frankie was . . . *looking at him*?!

She stood about ten feet away, staring right in his direction. Jaden straightened his baseball cap.

"Hey, Frankie," he said, trying to sound confident and charming.

Frankie waved.

"Be calm," Jaden whispered to himself. "Go talk to her. Make sure your hands aren't sweating."

"He's handsome," Frankie said. "Even with his braces."

Wait . . . what?

Jaden opened his mouth to speak —

— and was struck from behind by someone walking past.

"Excuse me, little dude," Luke said. He carried a tray of food, moving past Jaden and heading straight to Frankie.

"Hi, Luke," Frankie said, giving him another wave. "We want to sit in your section, so you'll be our waiter."

"Right this way, ladies." Luke led them toward a booth on the far side of the diner. They laughed and joked as they went.

Jaden's shoulders slumped. So much for thinking Frankie Dixon had even a second of time to spare for him. He spun on a heel and quickly fled the diner before any of his friends could stop him.

* * *

"Got your game face on?" Carlos asked the following morning as the four Snoops walked up the front steps of Fleischman Middle School. Fleischman was one of the oldest schools in the city. Even though it was Saturday, traffic crowded the streets around the cracked red-brick building.

Jaden nodded. "Ready," he said. A decent night's sleep had made him feel a little bit better about the science fair. He'd come to terms with the fact that he didn't have a shot at winning. But he was still going to enjoy blowing up his volcano.

The gymnasium was even more packed than it had been the night before. Many students were dressed up. Jaden saw Tariq in a button-down shirt and bow tie. Britt McDaniel was wearing a red dress that made her stand out in the crowd.

"I can't believe you talked me into dressing like this," Jaden mumbled to his sister. Jaden was dressed in a short-sleeved dress shirt and a tie with his favorite superhero, Action Man, on it.

"You look nice," Hayden said. She had on a striped shirt, matching skirt, and a pair of bright yellow sneakers.

"I feel weird." Jaden smoothed down his hair. He felt naked without his trusty baseball cap.

They reached their tables. Carlos and Keisha came over to Jaden's volcano and peered down at it. "This turned out great," Keisha said.

"Yeah," Carlos agreed. "I love the people. Nice touch."

Jaden shrugged.

"Huh," he heard Hayden say behind him. "That's weird."

Jaden turned to see his sister fidgeting with her tablet. "The application isn't loading." With each word she spoke, the fear in her voice grew. "If I can't get it up and running by the time the judges get here, I'll be disqualified."

"Where are my blueprints?" Britt's voice cut through the gym. She was scouring her table, searching the floor. "I had them in my backpack. Now they're gone. My whole backpack is missing!"

"Chip? Oh, for the love of . . . why isn't Chip working?" Sanjay Hurkadli had his headset on. He was trying to get his sleek robot to run and failing at it.

Jaden glanced from one table to the next. Hayden. Britt. Sanjay. They were all panicking, all dealing with science fair projects that weren't ready to show.

"Wait a second," Jaden said. "Something's not right. What's going on?"

That was when he heard the ticking. Low, nearly silent clicks. And they were coming from . . .

"My volcano!"

Jaden raced to his display, diving for the timer positioned on the back of it.

He was too late.

KER-SPLOOSH!

The model of Mount Vesuvius erupted in a geyser of thick, red lava. It hit Jaden right in the face, splattering him with goo!

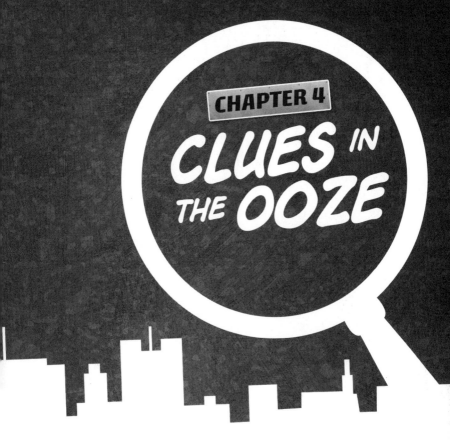

CHAPTER 4

CLUES IN THE OOZE

Drip. Drip. Drip.

Droplets of fake lava fell from the tip of Jaden's nose. It coated his hair and face and shirt. His Action Man tie was a goopy red mess. He stood there, horrified, while the crowd around him buzzed with whispers and giggles.

Jaden wiped the lava from his eyes just in time to see Hayden elbowing her way through the crowd. "Jaden!" she shouted.

"I'm fine," he answered before she asked. He felt like a volcano himself, the anger bubbling up inside like molten lava. How had the timer gone off? He hadn't set it, and he certainly wouldn't have made the eruption so strong.

"What happened?" Carlos asked.

"And why are you dripping with goo?" Keisha added.

"My volcano erupted," Jaden explained. He bent over to check the timer on the back. The small electronic device had been set to go off at 9:57 a.m. Jaden looked up at the gymnasium wall, where a large round clock enclosed in a cage of meshed metal read 9:58 a.m.

Someone had set the timer to purposely go off right before the competition.

"The science fair is about to start," Jaden said. "And my project is wrecked."

"Mine too," Hayden said. She'd moved up behind Keisha, holding her tablet. "The microchip that stores information from the application I built is missing."

"Missing?" Carlos looked from one twin to the other. "I smell a mystery. And . . . um, flowers?"

Jaden pointed at Britt McDaniel's table. "That's just Britt's alarm clock," he said. But then he saw Britt was still rummaging around her table.

"Have you still not found your backpack?" Jaden asked as he approached.

Britt looked up. "Agh!" she blurted out in shock. Then, shaking her head, she added, "Sorry. I saw your project explode. That sucks."

"Yeah." Jaden picked at the lava on his left cheek. It was starting to harden, making each smile and blink feel like he was slowly turning into a statue.

"Somebody took my backpack," Britt said. "It's the only explanation."

"And they took Chip's hard drive too." Sanjay Hurkadli stood with his hands on his hips. His robot sat on the table behind him, its back exposed. Wires snaked out of it.

"Whoa," Carlos said. "Hit the brakes. So all of your projects have been sabotaged in some way?"

The four kids glanced at one another, then nodded in unison.

"Looks like it," Hayden said.

"All right, science fair participants!" Principal Snider's voice echoed through the gym's speakers. "The competition is officially underway. Judges will be around to evaluate your projects. Good luck!"

"Well, that's it!" Sanjay threw his hands up in despair. "We're going to be disqualified."

"Let's just talk to Principal Snider," Hayden said. "I'm sure he'll understand."

"Understand what?" Sanjay countered. "That our projects are each missing parts? Or that they . . .," he gestured at Jaden, ". . . blew up in our faces?"

"We should still talk to him," Hayden said.

"Meanwhile, we have a mystery to solve. Snoops, Inc. is on the case," Carlos said.

While the group was arguing, Keisha had already begun searching the area around Jaden's table. She whistled and shouted, "Guys! Check it!" She dug into her pocket and retrieved her phone, then knelt down beside the table.

"Watch out for lava," Jaden said, noticing that his project was still oozing off the table. Some of Pompeii's plastic population were stuck in the muck or had fallen to the gym floor.

Keisha snapped a photo with her phone. She held it up for the others to see.

"Footprints," Jaden said. "Faint red footprints."

"Yep," Keisha said.

One of the prints was bigger than the others. It showed the dark red smear of half a shoe tread. The prints were behind Jaden's table, on the side where the timer was located.

"They're probably just mine." Jaden lifted his shoe to check his tread. Flecks of bright red goop were on it. "See?"

"It's not the same red color," Keisha noted. "These are darker."

While Britt dashed off to find Principal Snider, and Sanjay sulked at his table, the Snoops explored around Britt's table. They found nothing out of the ordinary. However, when searching the space around Hayden's project, Carlos came up with a clue.

"Look," he said, plucking two small, blue rubber bands from the floor. They were so tiny Jaden could hardly see them pinched between Carlos' fingers.

Jaden sighed to himself. This whole situation reminded him how the other Snoops had abilities

he didn't have. He never would have found the tiny bands, and he probably wouldn't have thought twice about the footprint.

Suddenly the vibe in the gymnasium shifted. Jaden looked up to see Tariq Washington strolling over. "What's all the commotion over here?" he asked, smugness in full effect. He saw Jaden and had to stifle a laugh. "Whoa. What'd I miss, Williams?"

"Our projects have been tampered with," Hayden explained calmly. Jaden balled his hands into fists. His belly felt like roiling lava again at the sight of Tariq's smile.

"That's lame," Tariq said. "Mine's just fine. In fact, the judges already looked at it. They were impressed, I could tell."

"It was you, wasn't it?!" Sanjay stepped forward. He held Chip in one hand, shaking his robot furiously. The exposed wires waved like tentacles.

"Heh. Looks like your Tin Man lost its heart, huh?" Tariq scoffed.

"You ruined all our projects!" Sanjay bellowed.

Before Tariq could respond, the normally cool and collected Sanjay dropped his robot and charged at Tariq!

CHAPTER 5

STATING THEIR CASE

With a growl of rage, Sanjay leaped at Tariq.

"What are you doing, man?!" Tariq shouted.

Sanjay didn't answer. Tears had formed in his eyes.

Jaden didn't have time to think; he needed to do something before a fight broke out.

"Hey!" Jaden yelled. "Knock it off!" He stepped in between the two angry boys.

Sanjay shoved him aside, and Jaden fell back onto the gym floor, right on his backside.

The crowd around them had turned toward the ruckus. Several parents began to step forward.

Keisha quickly wedged herself between Tariq and Sanjay. She successfully held Sanjay back. "It's not worth getting into a fight," she said calmly. Sanjay's breath was ragged as he wiped tears from his eyes with his fists. He snatched Chip off the gym floor before someone stepped on it.

"What's going on over here?"

The buzzing crowd parted as Principal Snider's voice thundered through the air. Britt walked quickly beside the principal, trying to keep up. Snider carried a clipboard in one hand.

"Nothing, sir," Keisha said. "Just a . . . disagreement." She turned her back on the principal, shooting a scowl at both Tariq and Sanjay. It was a look that said, *Don't you dare say a word, for your own good.*

"Humph." Principal Snider let out a sigh. "I should have known you kids would be involved."

Carlos stepped up to the principal. "Please," he said. "Something strange is going on. Someone seems to have sabotaged several of the science fair projects."

"Is that what happened to Williams there?" Principal Snider nodded at Jaden, whose goopy hair and clothes had now turned to crust.

"Nah," Jaden joked. "I just forgot to shower this morning."

Principal Snider was not amused.

"My volcano timer was turned on," Jaden explained, "and it turned me into a molten mess." He held out his spattered Action Man tie, then let it fall with a half-crunching, half-plopping sound.

"How exactly is your ill-timed explosion sabotage, Mr. Williams?"

Jaden filled the principal in on the whole story, showing him the timer set to 9:57 a.m. "I didn't leave it like that last night," he said. "Someone changed it."

The group took turns showing their ruined projects to the principal and the other judges who'd gathered around. But Jaden could see right away that Principal Snider wasn't buying it. They didn't have proof. Or a motive. Or even a suspect.

"Don't you see?" Sanjay pleaded when all of the kids had spoken. "The science fair should be postponed until the culprit is found."

Principal Snider mulled it over. Then, he shook his head. "I'm sorry," he said. "If you had proof that someone did this, action would definitely be taken. As it stands, though, I can't allow half-finished projects and I can't postpone the fair until they're complete. It wouldn't be fair to the rest of the students." The principal began to walk away. "If you'll excuse me, I need to return to judging the remainder of the projects."

Jaden watched Snider and the other judges continue on to the next table. Ironically, it featured a volcano that wasn't nearly as cool as his had been.

"Talk about not fair," Sanjay muttered.

"Well, this has been fun," Tariq said, adjusting his crooked bow tie. "But I should really get back to my table until the fair is over." He turned on one sneaker and breezed back down the row of tables to his own.

"I'm right, you know," Sanjay said. It took Jaden a moment to realize that the boy was speaking to him. "Tariq knows Hayden and I are the smartest kids in the class. Either one of us would have taken him down today."

He then held up his fingers to make air quotes, a move that really got under Jaden's skin. "If you 'detectives' want to find out who sabotaged our projects, there's only one real suspect." He began to gather his things, tearing down his trifold board with Chip's schematics on it and angrily closing it.

"Are you okay, Jaden?" Britt asked. She'd snuck up next to him. "You took a hard fall."

"Oh." Jaden tried to act calm, like his backside wasn't killing him. "I'm cool."

"Everyone's on-edge," she said. "I was already nervous before the competition. And now this. I barely slept last night . . . kept tossing and turning. I was still awake when Luke got home from work at midnight."

Just then Keisha nudged him. "Jaden," she whispered. "Follow me."

He excused himself.

"Look at Sanjay's table," Keisha said.

Jaden did. All he saw was parts and pieces and Chip lying facedown on the table, its exposed wires hanging out. What was he missing?

Sanjay sighed, then turned and headed off into the crowd, leaving his display half-destroyed. Keisha sidled up to the table, glancing in the direction Chip's creator went to make sure he wasn't returning.

She gestured for Jaden to join her. He did. "What is it?" he asked. They were alone; Britt McDaniel had wandered away to speak with a few of the other science fair participants.

Keisha was studying Chip carefully, afraid to touch him, like she thought the robot would pop up on its own and chase her away. She snapped a few photos with her phone.

Jaden leaned in close and finally saw what Keisha was excited about.

Among the stray nuts, bolts, and wires piled on the table by Chip was a handful of small rubber bands. They were a lot like the ones they'd found near Hayden's project!

CHAPTER 6

AND THE WINNER IS . . .

"No way," Jaden said. He stared first at the rubber bands on the table, then at the ones Keisha cradled in the palm of her hand.

"They aren't identical," Keisha said. "The ones I found are smaller and blue. But that doesn't mean they aren't from Sanjay's project."

"But you saw how he reacted when Tariq was here," Jaden said. "Heck, you had to hold them apart!"

Keisha shrugged her shoulders. "Maybe he was acting."

"Plus, if Sanjay was responsible, then why would he sabotage his own project?"

"I don't know," Keisha admitted. "Whatever the case, we should poke around his table a bit more. Come on."

"What are you doing?" Jaden and Keisha looked up to see Sanjay approaching. As he huffed over, Keisha quickly pocketed the rubber bands.

"Get away from my stuff," Sanjay demanded, shooing them off. "Chip has suffered enough damage already."

"Okay, cool." Jaden put his lava-crusted hands in the air. "We'll . . . uh . . . leave you two alone?"

He stumbled back. Keisha caught him, turning him around like a dancer until he faced the other Snoops. Hayden and Carlos, along with Britt McDaniel, had watched the whole ordeal.

"Sanjay's not usually so tightly-wound," Britt said.

"I get it," Carlos said. "Having your hard work taken apart like that. I'd be furious, too."

"That's just it," Britt said. "What you saw last night? Chip waving and saying hi? That's all it does."

"What do you mean?" Hayden asked.

"Sanjay's project was only half-finished. He told me himself. Yeah, he had grand plans for Chip. But he couldn't make everything work in time for the fair."

Jaden looked over at Sanjay's table, where the boy was placing Chip in a box along with the headset that controlled it. Would Sanjay really ruin other people's science fair projects just because he couldn't get his to work?

* * *

Jaden thankfully had a change of clothes in his gym locker. While the other Snoops stayed in the gym, he slipped off to the boys' locker room to change.

Fleischman students had nicknamed the locker room The Maze because of its odd construction. The room was broken into several areas — lockers, bathroom, showers — each with cracked concrete walls and not enough lights. Every movement echoed as Jaden wove down one long row of metal lockers, turned left, and down another.

His locker was near the back corner of the room. He quickly shed his crusty dress shirt. "Sorry, Action Man," he said with a sigh as he hung the dirty superhero tie on a hook.

When he came back out of the locker room, he was clean but still looked ridiculous. He wore a crumpled grey t-shirt with a cartoon image of a bulldog on it. His red shorts clashed dramatically with his black dress socks and dress shoes. And a few speckles of lava still coated his shoes. Still, he wasn't completely covered in goop, so he was going to call it a win.

A crowd had gathered near the front of the gymnasium. Principal Snider stood at the judges' table, a large blue ribbon in his hand.

"Jaden," Hayden whispered sharply. She and the other Snoops waved him over to join them.

"Stylin'," Carlos ribbed Jaden.

"Shut it." Jaden punched him lightly on the arm, silently thankful that Frankie Dixon wasn't there to see him. He'd probably fall over dead from embarrassment.

"Wow!" Principal Snider said. "What an amazing display of science-fair projects. The students here at Fleischman continue to excel, and I'm very proud of all of you."

Jaden was surprised to see Sanjay standing near the Snoops, arms folded across his chest. He thought the angry student would be long gone.

Principal Snider continued. "And now, to announce the winner of today's science fair. Drum roll, please." The other judges began rapping their knuckles lightly on the table.

"This young student's project — a solar-powered air heater — was spectacular. Ladies and gentlemen, today's science fair winner is . . . Tariq Washington!"

The crowd broke into applause. To Jaden, the outcome was not much of a surprise. Tariq's major competitors had been disqualified, and his win wasn't shocking.

Tariq, though, was floored. At least, he *acted* surprised. His jaw hung open as he walked up to Principal Snider.

"I'm . . . I'm speechless," Tariq said. He accepted the blue ribbon from the principal and held it up triumphantly.

"Boo!" Sanjay shouted, hands cupped around his mouth.

"Young man," Principal Snider began. "Please show a bit —"

Sanjay didn't give him time to finish his lecture. "BOO!" he shouted again, louder. Then he turned and disappeared back into the crowd.

"Guys," Hayden said, nudging Jaden with an elbow. "Check out Tariq's shoes."

Jaden glanced down at Tariq's sneakers. His left sneaker, to be exact. It was covered in red!

CHAPTER 7

A THIEF
IN THE
DARK

When the science fair award ceremony had concluded, the four Snoops made their way back to Jaden's table. His volcano, now just a crusty red pile of papier-mâché, was still standing by itself. None of the judges had even looked at it. He didn't even get a participation ribbon for it.

All that hard work . . .

As the Snoops began to discuss the baffling case, students around them tore down their projects and packed them up to take them home. Volunteers and teachers helped break down tables. Sanjay's table was empty.

"Okay," Carlos said. "So what have we got?"

Keisha brought out the rubber bands and placed them on the table. "These were found near Hayden's project," she explained. "And they look suspiciously like the kind Sanjay used to make Chip."

"What's his motive, though?" Carlos asked.

"His project didn't work the way he wanted it to," Keisha said. "So he ruined the others in the hopes that Principal Snider would postpone the science fair."

"Hmm. Its a stretch, but maybe." Carlos leaned against the table. "What else?"

"There was the red footprint by Jaden's table," Hayden said.

"And Tariq's tennis shoe, which had red goop on it," Jaden said.

"What's his motive?" Carlos asked.

"Jealousy," Hayden said. "Trying to knock myself, Sanjay, and Britt out of the competition to make his chances of winning easier."

Jaden noticed that his sister didn't mention him among Tariq's competition. That hurt a bit.

Jaden then saw Britt approaching her table to speak with a volunteer. Where did she fit into this whole thing? Why was her project affected? Come to think of it, why was his project ruined? It wasn't like his Vesuvius was gonna destroy the competition like its tiny plastic Pompeii residents.

A volunteer moved over to Sanjay's empty table to clean up. The old lady removed the tablecloth and began to fold it.

Britt gasped. "There they are!" She dropped to her knees and crawled under Sanjay's table. When she came out, a roll of long paper was clenched in one hand.

"It's her blueprints." Jaden quickly led the Snoops over to Britt's table.

"They were under Sanjay's table the whole time," Britt said, unrolling her schematics and double-checking to see if they were all accounted for. She seemed satisfied that they were.

"He must have stashed them under the table while he was sabotaging our projects," Hayden surmised.

"We gotta talk to him," Carlos said. "Sanjay just skyrocketed to become our prime suspect."

"But he left a while ago," Jaden said.

Britt shook her head. "I saw him outside a few minutes ago. He was sitting on the steps when I looked to see if Luke was here to pick me up."

"Come on," Carlos said. "Maybe it's not too late."

Jaden looked down at his terrible outfit. "Go on without me," he said. "I'm gonna duck into the locker room and get my dirty clothes."

The Snoops split up. Carlos led the girls toward the school's front entrance while Jaden hurried to the locker room.

It was still dark and empty inside The Maze. Jaden's dress shoes scuffed the locker room's cement floor with each step. He crumpled his clothes in a pile and shoved them under one arm. Then he took the Action Man tie and slung it around his neck.

Thud.

The sound came from somewhere in The Maze, and Jaden stopped in his tracks. He wasn't alone.

"Hello?" His voice bounced off the walls.

Footsteps hurried along from nearby. Jaden's heart hammered in his chest. Goosebumps crashed like waves along his arms and on the back of his neck.

"Hello?" he repeated. He grew more nervous by the second. "Sanjay? Tariq? Who's there?!"

The footsteps quickened, followed by the sound of the locker room door slamming open.

Jaden dashed forward, trying hard to catch up to the person. Whoever it was, they obviously didn't want to be caught in the locker room.

Jaden pushed open the door and hurried out into the darkened hallway. He looked left, then right.

There.

A figure was speed-walking down the hall. He or she wore a hoodie, and Jaden couldn't make out the person's identity.

But he could certainly make out what was slung over the figure's shoulder.

"Britt's backpack!" Jaden cried.

At the sound of his voice, the shadow turned, saw Jaden, and broke out in a full run down the hall. The figure quickly disappeared around the corner.

Jaden raced after the thief.

CHAPTER 8

RUNNING IN DRESS SHOES

The black dress shoes had been for his cousin's wedding. Jaden had wanted to wear his sneakers and baseball cap to the ceremony, but his mom had nixed that idea. So they'd spent a painfully long day at the mall. He'd come out of it with a suit coat he only wore the one time and the pair of black dress shoes he was wearing now. They were a size too big and made him feel like he was training to be a circus clown.

Jaden raced down the hall after the person carrying Britt's backpack. His clown shoes slapped loudly against the tile floor of Fleischman Middle School. Stumbling around a corner, Jaden burst through one of the school's side doors and into the bright sunlight. He squinted as his eyes began to water.

The backpack thief was running down the sidewalk, heading toward the nearest corner. Jaden leapt off the three stone steps and landed on the sidewalk.

"Jaden?" Hayden said, startled. She and the other Snoops stood at the opposite end of the building, by the school's main entrance.

"Guys! I found Britt's backpack!" He pointed at the hoodie-wearing thief dashing down the block. "He's got it! And he's getting away!"

Carlos and Keisha hurriedly spoke to one another. Then Keisha bolted toward Jaden, splitting the team in two. Her long, graceful strides made it look like she was practically gliding down the sidewalk.

Jaden took off in pursuit of the backpack thief with Keisha closing in on him. It felt weird running in something other than sneakers, and his clumsy footsteps were slowing him down.

He turned the corner just in time to see Hoodie Thief crossing the busy intersection ahead. Traffic was heavy; cars and trucks sat at the stoplight, bumper to bumper. A cement mixer rumbled loudly as it came to a stop.

Jaden lost sight of Hoodie Thief behind the cement mixer as the fleeing suspect turned left at the intersection and crossed the street.

"Where is he?" Keisha had caught up to Jaden. Of course she had.

Jaden pointed, racing to get to the intersection before the light changed.

Hoodie Thief was running toward a set of steps that led up to an elevated train platform.

"Hurry!" Keisha bolted across the street as the Don't Walk light began to blink. Jaden ran after her, making it through just before the light turned red. Behind him, the cement mixer roared to life as it accelerated.

Hoodie Thief took the platform steps two at a time. Even in the bright daylight, Jaden couldn't tell who they were chasing. The person was average sized, and the hooded sweatshirt covered the person's hair and face.

Keisha made it to the steps, easily bounding up them. Jaden put on a burst of speed and attempted to leap up the steps as well.

But his uncomfortable dress shoes made it hard. As he climbed, the toe of his left oversized shoe caught on a step. Jaden barely got his hands up in time before he fell face first into the steps.

"Oof!" The wind rushed from his lungs. A sharp pain shot through his left wrist, and he could feel the sting of scraped palms. Still, he pulled himself up, shaking his injured hands.

An older lady carrying two bags of groceries had stopped mid-way down the steps. "Are you all right, young man?" she asked.

Jaden grimaced. "Yes, mostly . . . ouch," he replied

The old woman shook her head and continued down the steps. "Kids," she said. "Always rushing to get somewhere."

Jaden carefully climbed the remainder of the steps and reached the top just as the doors of the elevated train dinged and closed. Keisha was further along the crowded platform. She was spinning in circles, scanning the crowd.

She'd lost the suspect. The train picked up speed and started to whoosh out of the station. Jaden looked toward the train as it passed, and suddenly saw Hoodie Thief standing by a window inside. He still couldn't see who it was — Tariq? Sanjay? — but he did notice one thing.

"He doesn't have the backpack anymore," Jaden said to himself.

But where had the burglar dropped it? Jaden remembered seeing it swinging from side to side as the thief climbed the platform steps.

Suddenly Jaden's stomach rumbled. The smell of hot dogs wafted over from the side of the platform. A street vendor with a bulky silver cart and a red umbrella was selling food to hungry customers. Jaden hadn't eaten anything since breakfast. Still . . .

"Not the time, fella," he said, patting his belly.

But as he watched the street vendor drop a juicy dog into a bun for a waiting customer, Jaden's stomach grumbled again. The delicious aroma of fresh-grilled hot dogs filled his nostrils. He couldn't help himself. Like a cartoon character following a delicious smell, Jaden walked toward the vendor.

But as he drew closer, a flash of pink to one side caught his attention. He looked over at the trash barrel again. There, perched on top of the trash like a pink prize, was Britt's backpack.

CHAPTER 9

NOT PIECING IT TOGETHER? THEN KETCHUP!

"Your stomach?" Carlos asked, bewildered. "You're saying your stomach helped you find the backpack?"

Jaden took a massive bite of his third foil-wrapped hotdog. "Yup," he said. "It's never steered me wrong." As he chewed, he added, "Well, except for that old shrimp I ate once. That was a bad move."

The Snoops were back at their office, a small storage unit in the basement of the apartment building where they all lived. The unit was one in a row with walls made of chain-link fencing. The office space was set up with a desk, a couple of chairs, a lamp, and a stray cat that liked to hang around while the young detectives discussed their mystery cases. They'd named the orange tabby cat Agatha. She was the team's unofficial mascot.

Jaden broke off a piece of hotdog and fed it to Agatha. The cat purred as she nibbled on the treat.

Britt's pink backpack sat in a pool of lamplight in the middle of the desk. Carlos, Keisha, and Hayden gathered around it. They hadn't opened it yet. After finding it, Jaden and Keisha brought it back to Fleischman. Britt had already begun to walk home, according to Hayden, so they hadn't gotten a chance to show her. The junior sleuths decided to head back to Snoops HQ to examine the evidence.

When they returned home, the other Snoops headed down to the office while Jaden ran upstairs

to hurriedly change his clothes. He felt almost
normal again after putting on his trusty ball cap.

"So are we gonna open it up and see what's
inside?" Jaden asked.

"It's not ours," Hayden said uncertainly. "That'd
be wrong. Right?"

"Wrong, right, whatever," Carlos said. "This
backpack could hold the key to the mystery. I'm
gonna open it."

Carlos carefully unzipped the backpack. Without
touching its contents, he lifted the pack and poured
them out.

Several items tumbled onto the desk:

- **Two battered paperback books from the
  Adoring Atlantis mermaid romance series.**
- **A geography textbook.**
- **A multi-colored headband.**
- **A hard drive . . .**
- **And a microchip.**

"Bingo," Carlos said.

Hayden popped the grape sucker she'd been
sucking on out of her mouth and pointed with it.

"That's the microchip for my tablet, the one with the data for my fingerprint application on it."

"And I'm guessing that's the hard drive from Sanjay's robot," Carlos said.

"So we can rule him out as a suspect," Keisha said. "Right?"

"Probably." Carlos sat in the lumpy desk chair and leaned back. "I mean, I suppose he could have stashed his own hard drive in the backpack. But if he did, then why would he leave Britt's blueprints under his table?"

"And then there's the rubber bands," Keisha added, dropping them onto the desk next to Hayden's tablet. "If they didn't come from Chip, then where did they come from?"

"What about Tariq?" Jaden asked. He took another big bite of his hot dog, licking ketchup from his lips.

"We found him outside the school, a few minutes before you ran out," Carlos explained. "The red stuff on his shoe wasn't on the bottom, just the top."

"It must have gotten on him when you tried to break up his argument with Sanjay," Hayden said.

Keisha placed her phone on the desk. On the screen was the photo of the red footprint. "Are you saying he didn't make these footprints then?" she asked.

"Doesn't look like it," Hayden said.

"Soooo . . . are we saying that neither of our suspects are suspects anymore?" Jaden asked.

The group sat in silence. Only the low sound of Agatha's purrs could be heard.

"Well," Jaden said, reaching for the hard drive on the desk. "Guess we can return this to Sanjay."

Just as his fingers were about to touch it, Hayden slapped them away. "Wait!" she shouted.

"Ow!"

"Sorry . . . not sorry." Hayden smiled. "I have an idea." She went to the office's dented file cabinet. Opening the bottom drawer, she took out what looked like a briefcase. Hayden brought it over to the desk and flicked the two latches on the side. "We're gonna do this old-school style."

"What is that?" Carlos asked. He slipped out of the lumpy chair and offered it to Hayden.

Inside the case, resting in small foam pockets, were things that looked to Jaden like they belonged in a make-up bag. Hayden removed a small glass container filled with white powder and a thin paintbrush with a fiberglass handle.

"It's my old fingerprint kit," Hayden said, waggling the brush in Jaden's face.

The Snoops watched as Hayden unscrewed the top of the powder case. She dipped the brush into it. "This is latent print powder," she explained, the sucker bouncing around in her mouth. "If there are any fingerprints on the hard drive, it will pick them up."

She lightly brushed the powder onto the hard drive. As she did, amazingly, Jaden saw several smudges appear. "Whoa," he whispered, leaning in to watch from over her shoulder.

"Gimme some room, Hot Dog Breath," Hayden said.

"Sorry," Jaden said. Then, blowing a long breath directed at Hayden, he added, "Not sorry."

"Eww."

Hayden took a roll of clear tape from the kit and pulled several small strips from it. "It looks like there's a couple of different sets of fingerprints on the hard drive," she said.

"How do you know?" Carlos asked.

"Every fingerprint has a different pattern of tiny ridges, valleys, and whorls."

"Like snowflakes," Keisha offered.

"Yep. Prints are more unique than DNA." While she spoke, Hayden pressed the small strips of tape to the different prints and stuck the tape on backing cards from the kit. "One of these prints has a high arch. The other has a thin, compact pattern called a simple loop."

She showed the Snoops the two cards. Jaden could see the difference right away. "Sure," he said. "But what are you gonna do? Take these to the police department so they can run a fingerprint check?"

"Nope." The sucker danced in Hayden's mouth. "Who needs the police?"

She plucked the microchip off the desk and inserted it into the tablet in front of her. A moment later, her science fair project glowed to life.

"Remember last night?" Hayden said. "A ton of kids tried this bad boy out. I'm guessing there's a good chance we'll find a match."

"It's worth a shot," Carlos said.

One at a time, Hayden placed the two prints against the tablet. The app scanned them. Then, after tapping several buttons with a flurry of fingers, Hayden sat back in the chair. It creaked as she placed her hands behind her head. "And now, we wait."

Jaden watched the tablet do its thing. It was amazing. If her project hadn't been ruined, Hayden would have brought home the blue ribbon for sure.

Without realizing it, Jaden slowly leaned over his sister's shoulder again. She brushed him back. "It's almost done," she said.

"Oh. Sure." As he backed up, a big glob of ketchup fell from his foil-wrapped dog. It landed right on Keisha's phone, which was still displaying the footprint photo.

"Watch it, Jaden," Keisha said.

"Sorry. Sorry." He swiped at the ketchup with one finger, wiping the screen clean.

And then, looking down at the ketchup and the photo of the red footprint, everything fell into place. The whole mystery made a strange kind of sense to him.

The rubber bands.

The red footprint.

The stolen backpack and missing blueprints.

"Guys," he said. "Maybe it's just the hot dogs talking, but I think I know who's responsible."

He laid it all out and made his case for the other Snoops. At first, Keisha laughed and Carlos questioned him. But when they were done discussing, they all agreed that Jaden's theory had to be right.

Just as they finished, and silence fell over the team, Hayden's fingerprint app dinged. She picked up the tablet. "We've got two hits," she said excitedly.

"Nice!" Carlos pumped a fist.

"The first set of prints belong to Sanjay," Hayden said. "Which, you know, makes sense. It's his hard drive and all."

"Well?" Keisha pressed. "What about the other set? Who do they belong to?"

Hayden looked at her twin brother and smiled.

CHAPTER 10

THE *TRUTH IS OUT THERE*

It was close to lunch the following day when the Snoops, Inc. team reached their destination. They sat on an old wooden bench near the sidewalk. Pedestrians bustled by on either side of them, walking their dogs or getting groceries or eating lunch with friends and family.

The city never stopped moving; it was always alive with activity, and Jaden loved it. Each night, he kept the window to his and Hayden's bedroom cracked open, right near his bunk, so he could feel like he was a part of it. Each morning, he woke to find one of his parents had closed it.

"You sure you got the time right?" Carlos asked, perched on the back of the bench.

"Yep," Jaden said. "She told me that they'd be here."

Sure enough, moments later, the two people they were waiting for rounded the corner. They stopped in front of the doors to Burger BOOM! where the Snoops gang were waiting for them.

It was Britt McDaniel and her brother Luke. Luke was wearing his work uniform.

"Why'd you wanna walk me to work?" Luke asked his sister. He stopped, and seeing the junior sleuths waiting, said, "Oh. Hey guys."

"S'up, Luke," Carlos said.

"What's going on?" Luke asked Britt.

Britt shrugged. "I have no idea," she said. "Jaden just asked me about your schedule and said to come with you."

"Why?" Luke responded.

"Maybe because it's easier to talk to someone when they aren't running away from you," Jaden said.

"Good one," Hayden whispered to him.

"Thanks," he whispered back.

A look of surprise crossed Luke's face. Then, just as quickly, it was gone. "What are you even talkin' about, dude?"

"Oh, I think you know. You sabotaged the science fair projects," Carlos stated casually.

"What?" Britt was genuinely shocked.

"That's dumb," Luke said. "Why would I do that?"

"So your sister could win," Keisha said.

A tiny gasp escaped Britt's lips as she looked over at her brother. "Seriously?" she asked.

"Pffft . . . ," Luke snorted. "I think you're forgetting something. Britt didn't win the stupid science fair. Nice work. You're a real smart bunch of private eyes."

"The only reason her project was ruined is because you forgot about her blueprints," Carlos explained. "Her project was the only one in the area that wasn't touched. You didn't mean to ruin her chances of winning. But her blueprints slipped out of her backpack when you used it to stash Hayden and Sanjay's hardware."

"We're not sure why you didn't destroy everyone else's projects too," Keisha said. "Maybe because that'd be too suspicious. So you decided to take out the ones you knew were serious threats."

"The only reason you missed Tariq's project was because he came to set up late, after you'd already left for work," Hayden added sternly.

"What a stretch." Luke turned to the door of Burger BOOM! and reached out to grab the handle. "Get back to me when you've got some solid proof."

"Oh, you want proof?" Hayden asked. "Here's your backpack, Britt."

Luke spun around as Hayden tossed the pink pack to its owner. His eyes were like saucers.

"Yeah," Jaden said. "My nose found it after you ditched it on the train platform."

"Now that we've got your attention," Carlos said. "Let's run it down. Shall we?"

He started by bringing out the tiny rubber bands he'd found near Hayden's table. "I'm guessing you use the same ones on your braces," he said. "Give us a smile."

Luke, suddenly self-conscious, closed his mouth tight and shook his head.

"Then there was this." Keisha showed him the photo of the footprint. "We found them by Jaden's exploded volcano."

"They're ketchup footprints, aren't they?" Jaden asked. "Like the kind someone working at a diner could get on their shoes. I should have recognized it. Food is my thing, you know? But the splatters of lava threw me off."

Luke toed the sidewalk with one sneaker. He kicked a rock off into the road. "Like I said, I don't know what you're talking about. I wasn't even close to the science fair yesterday."

"But you didn't need to be," Carlos said. "Because you sabotaged it the night before. You got off work and snuck into the school in the dark. You stashed the backpack at the school to keep Britt from finding it at home. Then you went back for it after the fair was over, when you were coming to pick her up. I'm guessing you were going to ditch the goods somewhere and give her the backpack, saying she left it at home."

"But then Jaden saw you," Keisha said. "So you ditched the whole thing in the trash."

Jaden walked over to the Burger BOOM! door and pointed at the sign indicating the restaurant's hours. "Closing time is ten o'clock," he said. "But Britt said she was still awake when you got home . . . after midnight."

"So where'd you go after work, Luke?" Keisha asked.

Defeat washed over the teenager's face and body. His shoulders slumped. "Fine," he said. "I'm sorry. I just . . . I wanted to level the field a bit, give Britt a chance to shine."

"By cheating?!" Britt was furious. "Thanks a lot, Luke."

"Hey, I didn't know about the missing blueprints."

"I don't care about the blueprints!" She shoved her brother in the chest with both hands. "I care that you didn't have any faith in me, like I couldn't do this without my big brother's help."

"Yeah." Luke was quiet. "Yeah, I deserve that. I'll . . . I'll talk to your principal, tell him the truth. I don't know, maybe he'll give you a second chance to show off your projects."

"Thanks," Hayden said.

"I . . . I gotta go to work." Luke sullenly shoved open the door of Burger BOOM! and walked inside to start his shift. Britt remained outside with the Snoops, standing in silence.

Finally, she said, "Well, thanks . . . I guess. And sorry about my brother."

Jaden looked at his sister. "No problem. I get it. I'd do anything for my sister, too."

Hayden batted her eyes jokingly and said, "Awwww. What a guy."

"You're ruining the moment," Jaden said.

"Awwww," Hayden teased.

"Fine. I take it back."

"Looks like we closed another case," Carlos said. He nodded his head at the bustling diner. "How about we have a celebratory lunch?"

There was no hesitation. "Yep," Jaden said. "I could eat." He rushed to the door, swung it open, and ushered Britt and the other Snoops inside the diner.

"You can always eat," Hayden said as she passed him.

It was true. Hayden was the brains of Snoops, Incorporated. Keisha was the brawn. Carlos was the charm. That meant Jaden was the stomach — and he was cool with that.

Jaden shrugged. "What can I say? It's my gift."

THE END

Snoops, Inc. Case Report #003

Prepared by Jaden Williams

THE CASE:

Find out who ruined a bunch of science fair projects, including my awesome Mt. Vesuvius that spewed lava all over me. *ALL . . . OVER . . . ME*! (It was gross.)

CRACKING THE CASE:

Hayden's project was a fingerprinting application. She told me how everyone has ridges, loops, and spirals on their fingertips. They're never alike, even if you're identical twins!

Sweat glands in our fingers ooze oils, so whenever we touch something, it leaves an imprint that we often can't see. Police use methods like brushing powder on objects to make fingerprints visible. Then they use computer programs to match the prints to possible suspects.

Fingerprints have other uses too. Many people use their own prints to securely access things like cell phones, computers, and high security buildings. People in some countries even use their thumbprints as their signature.

Hayden's fingerprint app, PrintFinder Xtreme, and her old-school fingerprinting kit were critical for solving this mystery. Without them (and my trusty stomach), we wouldn't have been able to . . .

CRACK THE CASE! _

WHAT DO YOU THINK?

1. The Snoops take cases without worrying about getting paid for their time. Why? What motivates them to solve mysteries?

2. Hayden uses a fingerprint application to discover the culprit's identity. What are some other methods detectives use to catch criminals?

3. Jaden has difficulty finding out how he fits into Snoops, Incorporated. If you were on a detective team, what skills would you be able to offer? How would you help the team?

WRITE YOUR OWN!

1. Imagine that you're taking part in your school's science fair. Design your project by both describing it and drawing a blueprint for it.

2. Sanjay and Tariq are bitter rivals in this story. Write separate stories about their conflict from Sanjay's perspective, and then Tariq's. What changes between the two stories?

3. Imagine that you are Principal Snider and that you feel bad for the students whose projects were ruined. Write a letter to the disqualified students, apologizing and offering them a second chance.

GLOSSARY

BLUEPRINT (BLOO-print)—a detailed plan for a project or an idea

CULPRIT (KUHL-prit)—someone who is guilty of doing something wrong or of committing a crime

MICROCHIP (MYE-kroh-chip)—a tiny circuit that processes information in a computer

PANIC (PAN-ik)—a sudden feeling of great terror or fright

PAPIER-MÂCHÉ (PAY-pur muh-SHAY)—paper that has been soaked in glue used for making models and other crafting projects

PARANOID (PAIR-uh-noyd)—having an unreasonable feeling that people do not like you or may try to harm you

SABOTAGE (SAB-uh-tahzh)—to damage, destroy, or interfere with something on purpose

SCHEMATIC (skih-MA-tik)—a simple drawing or diagram that shows the parts of something

ABOUT THE AUTHOR

Brandon Terrell has been a lifelong fan of mysteries, shown by his collection of nearly 200 Hardy Boys books. He is the author of numerous children's books, including several titles in series such as Tony Hawk's 900 Revolution, Jake Maddox Graphic Novels, Spine Shivers, and Sports Illustrated Kids: Time Machine Magazine.

When not hunched over his laptop, Brandon enjoys watching movies and television, reading, watching and playing baseball, and spending time at home with his wife and two children in Minnesota.

ABOUT THE ILLUSTRATOR

Mariano Epelbaum is an experienced character designer, illustrator, and traditional 2D animator. He has been working as a professional artist since 1996, and enjoys trying different art styles and techniques.

Throughout his career Mariano has created many expressive characters and designs for a wide range of films, TV series, commercials, and publications in his native country of Argentina. In addition to Snoops, Inc., Mariano has also contributed to the Fairy Tale Mixups and You Choose: Fractured Fairy Tales series for Capstone.

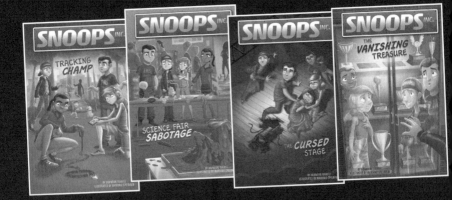